I'm New Here

Anne Sibley O'Brien

Charlesbridge

For Grace Valenzuela and the staff at the Multilingual & Multicultural Center of Maine's Portland Public Schools, who daily build bridges for children to cross, from one world to another

Acknowledgments

I express my heartfelt thanks to the people who provided crucial information and personal and technical support throughout the development of this book: Marty Braun, Kirsten Cappy, Mohammed Dinni, Shamso Farah, Mahmoud Hassan, Margy Burns Knight, Judy Lowell-Riley and her Ocean Avenue third graders, O. B. O'Brien, Virginia Marie Rincon, Taz Sibley, and Linda Ward.

And to the collaborative team at Charlesbridge: my editor, Julie Bliven, and designer, Whitney Leader-Picone, with support from Yolanda Scott and Susan Sherman. This book wouldn't have been possible without you.

First paperback edition 2018
Copyright © 2015 by Anne Sibley O'Brien
All rights reserved, including the right of reproduction in whole or in part in any form. Charlesbridge and colophon are registered trademarks of Charlesbridge Publishing, Inc.

Published by Charlesbridge
85 Main Street,
Watertown, MA 02472
(617) 926-0329
www.charlesbridge.com

Illustrations done in watercolor on Arches 60-lb. watercolor paper and colored digitally
Display type set in Hunniwell by Aah Yes Fonts
Text type set in Tonic by Tomi Haaparanta
Color separations by Colourscan Print Co Pte Ltd, Singapore
Printed by C & C Offset Printing Co. Ltd.
    in Shenzhen, Guangdong, China
Production supervision by Brian G. Walker
Designed by Whitney Leader-Picone

Library of Congress Cataloging-in-Publication Data
O'Brien, Anne Sibley, author, illustrator.
    I'm new here / by Anne Sibley O'Brien.
        pages cm
    Summary: Three children from other countries (Somalia, Guatemala, and Korea) struggle to adjust to their new home and school in the United States.
        ISBN 978-1-58089-612-2 (reinforced for library use)
        ISBN 978-1-58089-613-9 (softcover)
        ISBN 978-1-60734-776-7 (ebook)
        ISBN 978-1-60734-775-0 (ebook pdf)
1. Immigrant children—United States—Juvenile fiction. 2. Assimilation (Sociology)—Juvenile fiction. 3. Somalis—Juvenile fiction. 4. Guatemalans—Juvenile fiction. 5. Koreans—Juvenile fiction. [1. Immigrants—Fiction. 2. Assimilation—Fiction.] I. Title.
PZ7.O1267Iab 2015
813.6—dc23   2013049031

Printed in China
(hc) 10 9 8 7
(sc) 10 9 8 7 6 5 4 3 2 1

I am new here.

I am new here.

We have a new student, everyone. Her name is Fatimah.

Back home I knew the language.

My friends and I talked all day long.

Our voices flowed like water and flew between us like birds.

Here there are new words.

I can't understand them.

The sounds are strange to my ears.

Back home I could read and write.
I shaped the letters and stacked them like blocks into words.
The words opened like windows and doors into a story.

Here there are new letters.

They lie on the page like scribbles and scratches.

All the windows and doors are shut tight.

Back home I was part of the class.

I knew just what to do.

I fit in like one of many stars in the night sky.

Here there are new ways.

I cannot see the patterns.

I cannot find my place.

Here I am alone.

Here I am confused.

Here I am sad.

I **say** the new words again and again.

They feel like rocks in my mouth.

My tongue twists and stumbles on their edges.

One day I try new words.
They do not flow or fly freely.
But someone understands.

I am finding new friends.

And they are finding me.

I write the letters over and over.

I stare at the words.

I look for a way to open them.

One day I write some new letters.
They are not perfect.
But I can read the words.

I **watch** the new ways more and more.

I try to see the patterns.

I am scared I will make a mistake.

One day I try taking part.
My knees tremble, and my heart pounds.
But my teacher smiles.

I am sharing with others.
And they are sharing with me.

Fatimah, you're a really good artist.

Here there are new beginnings.

Here there is a place for me.

Here is a new home.

A Note from the Author

When I was seven years old, my family traveled halfway around the world to live in a country brand-new to us. As white Americans in postwar South Korea, where my parents served as medical missionaries, we were welcomed with great courtesy and generosity. My siblings and I attended international schools where lessons were in English—our first language.

Even so, adjusting to living in a new culture and learning a new language was often challenging. I still remember moments when I felt bewildered and out of place. Over time, though, Korea became our beloved second home.

Today I see that the children of new Americans face far greater challenges than I ever did. Each difference they must navigate—including language, culture, race, and religion—adds one more layer of difficulty to their experience. In a foreign school culture, immigrant children who don't speak English must relearn to read, write, and speak in a new language. Many go through a silent phase as their brains process all this new information.

Additionally, the reasons for and the losses incurred in leaving home countries add to the challenges of building a new life. Children like Jin may have left behind close family members. Other families, like Maria's and Fatimah's, may have left home not by choice but by force, fleeing from political persecution, violence, or war. Classmates, teachers, and neighbors can assist these new Americans through their transitions by offering smiles, encouraging words, patience, and kind gestures, and by listening to their stories.

One way to help create a welcoming community is through sharing books. **I'm Your Neighbor**—a project that promotes children's literature featuring new arrivals—includes an extensive list of recommended titles at **www.imyourneighborbooks.org**. Seeing themselves reflected in these books, immigrant children feel affirmed, and their classmates glimpse different backgrounds and experiences—perhaps recognizing some of their own stories in the universals of family, traditions, journeys, and the quest for a better life.